A Marine's Second Chance

Marine for You/SEALed for You Crossover Novella

Marissa Dobson

Published by Dobson Ink
Printed in the United States of America
ISBN-13: 978-1-939978-93-6

Dedication:

To all the military spouses.

Contents

Married life hadn't been everything that Wyoming Dorset dreamed of. She thought she knew what she was getting into when she fell in love with a Marine. Training and deployments were the least of their problems. What she couldn't deal with was the distance that Jeffrey put between them. Only a shell of the man she fell in love with stood before her.

Five years—that's how long they'd been married. As Jeffrey prepared for another deployment, he thought of Wyoming and wondered how much of their marriage he'd been there for. How much had he been gone for? The divide between them seemed to appear overnight and now he wasn't sure how to fix it.

When unexpected news arrived hours before his deployment, somehow he convinced her to give him a second chance. She doesn't know why, but he believes that even with miles separating them, he can convince her that they haven't lost their chance. She's not sure if she believes him, but he'll be back in six months. That isn't too long to wait for her husband.

Chapter One

Pregnant? Wyoming Dorset sat there staring at her husband, waiting for him to say something. Saying anything would be better than silence. This would have been happy news if it was earlier in their marriage, but now…now she didn't know. Their marriage was on shaky ground, and the wall he threw up between them became thicker with every deployment. How did this happen? They had taken precautions. She was on the pill, never missing a day even when he was gone, because she never knew when he'd return.

"Damn it, Jeffrey, say something." She couldn't take the silence any longer. If he was angry, then she wanted him to rage. If he was happy about the pregnancy, she needed to hear it. Whatever was going through his mind, she needed to know because the silence was torture.

"I…" He dropped his bag on the bed. "How far along are you?"

"Don't you dare, Jeffrey! You might not give a shit about me or this child, but don't you dare ask me to have—"

"Is that what you think? That I don't care about you?" In a quick stride he came around the bed and touched the side of her face, caressing her cheek. "Damn it, Wyoming, that couldn't be further from the truth."

"You have a funny way of showing it." She fought against the instinct to press against his hand and enjoy the sweet caress. How long had it been since he'd touched her like that? How long had it been since the romance left their relationship? She could pinpoint the date and time she noticed the first change in him, but how had she let it get so bad?

"Wyoming, I—"

This time, she cut him off. She couldn't take one more excuse, or another one of his halfhearted apologies. "It doesn't matter. Things changed and we're just too different now. It's too late, but please don't ask me to have an abortion. Let me hold on to some respect for you." She took a deep breath because the moment she feared was there in front of her, and nothing could stop the outcome. "You don't have to worry about it. We'll be gone when you get back."

"Fuck!" Dropping his hand away from her cheek, he took a step back.

The absence of his touch made her heart ache. Even after everything, she still loved him. Tears pricked behind her eyelids, and she blinked them away. There was plenty of time for tears later, but she refused to cry in front of him. She didn't want him to stay out of pity, or because of the pregnancy. Love and romance, that's what she wanted.

He stepped back farther until the back of his legs brushed along the edge of the bed and he sat down, letting out a deep sigh. "That's not what I want. Abortion never crossed my mind."

"Then why ask how far along I am?" Maybe she jumped to a conclusion without giving him a chance, but it was the first thing that popped into her thoughts.

"It's September. If you conceived six weeks ago, that would be July." He glanced up at her, the corners of his lips pulling into a smile. "Everyone in my family who got pregnant in July had a girl. But if you're further along…"

"Nine weeks, but it will be a few weeks before we know the sex."

10

"Stay." He shot off the bed and came to stand in front of her. "Don't leave. This mission shouldn't take long, and I'll be back soon."

"I don't know." She wanted him to wrap his arms around her and tell her that everything would be fine. It wasn't that simple, especially not between them. She had a stable career, and she could provide for her and the child if he wasn't in the picture. Would she have considered leaving him if a child wasn't involved? She wasn't sure. Their relationship had been shaky for more than a year but she hadn't thought of divorce until she found out she was pregnant. There was no way she wanted to raise a child in a house filled with the tension that surrounded them. *I'm doing this for you, little one.* But was it the right thing?

"Even if you don't anymore, at one time you loved me," he said. "We owe it to our child to find that love again." He took her hand in his and dragged his thumb across her wedding band. "My feelings for you haven't changed. They're still the same as the day I put this on your finger. I know I haven't been the best husband, but let me prove to you that I want you in my life. I can be the man you need me to be. I can be the father to our daughter that she deserves. Don't give up on me."

"We've got to go, you need to be at—"

"Screw it," he snapped. "Damn it, Wyoming. I love you. I'm an asshole and I don't deserve you, but that doesn't mean I don't want you."

Tears filled her eyes and this time she couldn't blink them away. She wanted things to be different, but wasn't it too late for them? Did they have a chance to fix whatever was broken between them? Could they do it before the baby was born? She wanted her child to grow up surrounded by love.

"Don't cry, baby." He wrapped his arms around her and pulled her tight against his chest. "I never wanted to be the reason you cry. If you don't love me, I'll support your decision but—"

"Damn it, Jeffrey." Tears came faster and her chest tightened. "Loving you was never the problem. I've always loved you."

"Then stay." He loosened his embrace and leaned back so that she could look at him. "Give me time to prove to you that I can be the man you need, and a good father to our child. We'll make this right. Give me a chance."

"It's not always that easy." She took him in and tried to decide if he was willing to listen to her, or if he'd shut her out again and close off communication like he always did when she tried to talk to him about something like this. "There's a wall between us now, and every time I try to breach it, you reinforce it. We never even talk anymore. You always made me laugh but now…" *There's only tears.* She couldn't bring herself to say the last part. It wasn't only his fault. Maybe she could have done something different, something to get him to open up to her.

"Give me another chance." He cupped the side of her face, brushing his thumb along her cheek, wiping away the tears. "The man who made you laugh is still there, just buried, but I can find him again. This deployment is short. I'll be back before you know it and I'll prove it to you. Stay, baby."

She wanted to believe him. She wanted the man she fell in love with back again. Was it possible? She didn't know, but she was willing to give it a chance. Maybe she was clinging to her dream of the perfect family, but she believed their son or daughter deserved to have both parents. She wanted the happy family home she'd envied as a child. A mother and father who actually got along, the two and a half kids, and the white picket fence. "I'll be here when you get back." She could give him that long and see how things went.

"Promise?"

"Yes." She met his gaze and nodded. After five years of marriage, they deserved this chance. She wasn't willing to throw away all their time together, their memories, and the love she had for him if he was willing to try. "Now, we should get on the road."

"I promise you're not going to regret this decision." He pulled her back against him. "I love you, Wyoming. Things are going to be different, I promise."

She wrapped her arms around him, returning his embrace. How long had it been since they shared an embrace like that? In her gut, she knew the answer—just before he'd deployed a year ago. Just before the change in him. Since then, any time they held each other, it was short and his body felt stiff. He closed her out. Maybe he'd do it again, but she had to give him the benefit of the doubt that this time would be different. "I love you, too."

Chapter Two

The volunteer deployment had seemed like the perfect opportunity when Jeffrey agreed, but he hadn't realized how much his life would change just hours before he shipped out. Six months seemed like nothing when he signed the paperwork, but now that Wyoming was pregnant it felt like an eternity. He had so much to prove to her, and the distance between them would only make that harder.

Until the words came out of her mouth that she would be gone before he got back, he hadn't realized how close he came to losing her. She was everything to him. Before boarding his flight, he clung to her longer than normal, reminding himself that she'd be there when he returned. This wasn't goodbye. Six months…he'd be back before the birth of their child. Now that the plane was in the air, he couldn't shake the weight on his shoulders or the knot in his gut. Maybe he was overthinking things, but his gut told him that this deployment wasn't going to be a walk in the park. He'd have to fight hard to make it back to her. *If I make it back to her…no, when I make it back…I'm done.*

His commitment to the Marines was up in ten months and he wasn't reenlisting. Before he found out that she was pregnant, he had planned to. It was why he volunteered for this deployment. Advancement in his career.

Becoming a father would change things. He wanted to be there to see his child grow and he didn't want to miss all the things his own father missed while he was growing up. No, Jeffrey wanted to be there when his child took his first steps, said his or her first word, and he wanted to be there with Wyoming. They'd find a way through the darkness that had surrounded him since he returned from his last deployment.

He was willing to admit to himself, if to no one else, that his last deployment changed him. Something snapped within him and what he saw overseas plagued his dreams. Too many of his buddies were injured or dead due to bad intelligence. How he'd managed to walk away unharmed was something he couldn't understand.

He made it home to Wyoming because of Gunnery Sergeant Lucky Diamond. They drove right into a trap, but Lucky got them out alive. Most of them, but not everyone, made it. Memories of that mission filled his thoughts as he leaned back against the airplane seat.

Gunfire broke out in nearly every direction and they were sitting ducks in the middle of the road. He was taking in the situation, looking for possible routes to keep them alive, when Gunnery Sergeant Diamond's voice crackled over the radio. "Reverse. Fall back. Now!"

With another Humvee behind them, he hoped they heard the orders and their escape hadn't been closed off. As soon as he had the clearance, he swung left and turned the Humvee around, gunning it back the way they came, with the third Humvee in their caravan now leading the way. They were taking some gunfire, but the insurgents seemed to be focusing more on Lucky's Humvee, which had been the lead vehicle. One minute the gunshots were deafening, and then the next the assault subsided. Johnson's machinegun fired the only continuing shots.

Had they won? Was it winning if they were retreating to safer grounds? No, it was living to fight another day. He pressed his foot against the pedal a little harder, hoping to put more distance between them. They needed to get somewhere safe and regroup. The battle was ending but the war wasn't over. Regrouping…

A bomb exploded, shaking the road under his wheels and for the moment he had to make sure he hadn't run over an IED. It wasn't until he checked the mirror that he realized what happened. Gunny's Humvee sailed through the air for what seemed like an eternity before landing on its side with a thump, thirty feet from where it had been. Something else sailed through the air. What was it?

"Fuck!" Johnson hollered from the turret, where he was returning fire.

There was no doubt in his mind that Johnson had seen the same thing. One of their comrades had been thrown from the Humvee, to land hard, and now wasn't moving. Whoever it was might not be alive but they had to do something.

"Dorset!" Doc, their corpsman, dug into his field bag, preparing to respond.

"I know." Jeffrey slammed his foot down on the break. "Johnson, watch our backs and shoot anything that moves."

He grabbed his rifle from the rack near the door hinge and headed to assist. Doc needed to patch up whoever was still alive and they needed to get out of there before the insurgents opened fired on them again.

"Shit, it's Phillips." Even from this distance he could recognize Private First Class Phillips. Blood spilled along the sand, coming faster than it could be absorbed, making him wonder if Phillips was even alive.

With a jerk of his head, Jeffrey let go of the memories, but he couldn't shake the images of Kyle Phillips's mangled body. The young Private First Class had been new to their unit and with his presence he brought a new ray of hope. He was lighthearted and happy-go-lucky, something the whole unit needed.

Refusing to allow the memories of the last deployment to set the tone for this one, he turned his thoughts to his wife and unborn child. If he had to, he'd fight harder to make it home to them. He was going to be there when his child was born, and he wouldn't be like his absent father. He'd be in their life from the beginning, never missing an event, and making sure they knew he was always there if they needed him. He'd prove to Wyoming that the love they shared was still there and strong. *How? I don't know, but I'll do it.*

* * *

The first day of a deployment always seemed to be the hardest for Wyoming. Other wives felt the opposite, that they could picture their spouse on duty, so the first day wasn't as difficult. That it was later in the deployments that things became harder. For her, the minute she walked through the front door of their house, it sank in that it was the first of many days she'd be alone.

She sank down on the sofa and stared up at their wedding picture. It was a simple affair with a justice of the peace marrying them in a nearby park. Their parents, her sister, and a couple friends were there to witness their special day. Everything was so perfect, giving her the hope it would always be that way.

"I miss the way things used to be." She grabbed the throw pillow and hugged it to her chest, thinking of the early days of their marriage when he returned home at the end of the day and they couldn't keep their hands off each other. The sex had always been good, but back then they'd cuddle in bed or on the sofa as they watched a movie. Now he sat in the recliner, leaving her alone on the sofa. In bed, he stuck to his side of the mattress and kept his back to her. The lines between them were drawn firmly, making her doubt that things would be different when he returned.

Our parents. Dread settled over her shoulders. With him gone, she was left to tell them the news of her pregnancy alone. Having family get-togethers were never the highlight of her day. They always seemed to turn into a disaster as her parents couldn't even stand to be in the same room together, let alone get through a whole meal peacefully. Her mother-in-law didn't make the situation easier by butting in with her comments about how she'd never put up with the way Wyoming's father treated her mother. Halfway through dinner, she was ready to scream for everyone to get out, but Jeffrey always had a way of keeping the situation under control.

"Maybe I can video chat them?" She wasn't sure it was the best way to tell them, but it certainly was the least stressful. Before she had time to consider it further, her cell phone beeped, alerting her to a text.

Come for dinner? 6? I'll chill the wine. Her best friend Alessa, already reminding her that she wasn't alone. Both military spouses, they stuck together when their husbands deployed. Being in the same unit, they were normally gone together, giving her peace of mind knowing that Jeffrey had someone watching his back. It also kept her from feeling like a third wheel.

Needing to be alone, she shot back a quick text. *Thanks, but another night. I'm tired. Lunch tomorrow—usual place.*

Before she could set her phone down, a reply came through. *See you then.*

With a smile, she put the phone aside and stretched out on the sofa. Before she told their parents or her sister, she'd tell Alessa. Even though Alessa and Steve had been trying to get pregnant for the last two years, she knew her best friend would be happy for them. *Happier than my parents.*

Chapter Three

Searching design ideas online for the nursery had sucked Wyoming's time until she realized how late it had gotten. She dashed around the house, trying to get ready for her lunch date with Alessa when the doorbell rang. Figuring it was a package, she ignored it and leaned closer to the mirror as she added her mascara, only to have the annoying bell ring again.

"Damn it." She shoved the mascara brush back into the tube and headed for the door. She had to leave in ten minutes and she hadn't even blow-dried her hair yet. "This better be good," she mumbled to herself as she tugged open the door.

"Thank heavens you're here." Dakota brushed past her and dropped a duffle bag onto the floor next to the coffee table. "I can't take them a minute longer. All they do it fight and nothing I do is ever good enough."

"Well, hello to you too." She shut the front door and eyed her sister. "You're eighteen, so move out."

"I did…I mean, I am. I just need a place to stay for a couple of days." Dakota dropped onto the sofa and let out a heavy sigh. "Please, Wyoming, I can't go back there."

Knowing the kind of hell it was living with their parents, she nodded. "Fine, but I'm inviting them over for dinner on Saturday. Mom, Dad, and

Mr. and Mrs. Dorset. If you're staying here, you'll have to help keep everyone from fighting during dinner. Afterward, I'll kick them all out and they can fight on the front lawn if they have to."

"After the last family dinner, you're going to do it again? Without Jeffrey here? Are you insane?" Without looking away, she tugged her hair back into a messy ponytail. "That's a worse deal than sleeping in my car."

"I'm doing it because...never mind. Forget it." She tugged her cellphone out of the back pocket of her jeans and pulled up the earlier string of text messages from Alessa. *Change of plans. Could you come here instead? Dakota's here, been fighting with our parents. I'll prepare something.*

"Tell me." Dakota's voice was too close to a whine for Wyoming to handle at the moment, making her cringe.

Before she could deal with her sister, Alessa replied. *I'll pick up food and be there.*

"Are you even listening to me?"

"Damn it, D." She shoved her phone back into the pocket of her jeans and glanced at her sister. "Don't think you can come into my house and start acting like a brat. I know it's hell living with Mom and Dad, but I don't need you being whinny."

"You're never like this. What's wrong? Is it because of Jeffrey again? Maybe it's time for you to leave him."

"Leave him out of this." Wyoming had enough of everyone thinking they knew what was good for her. Ever since she told her mother about Jeffrey's deployment, she'd heard nothing except rude comments. *If you want a man who's going to stick around, you need to start dating.* Dating? Was her mother serious? She was married and even through all of their problems, she took her marriage vows seriously. Her mother might not, but she sure as hell did.

"What has you so moody?"

Letting her sister's words sink in, she came around to sit in Jeffrey's chair. "I'm pregnant."

"What?" Dakota's mouth dropped open.

"Not the reaction I was hoping for." But what could she honestly expect? If there was one person she confided in besides Alessa, it was Dakota. There was a six-year age gap between the two of them, but they had always been best friends. If there was any distance between them now, it was only due to the fact she didn't understand the relationship she had with Jeffrey. When it came to her relationship, it was easier to talk to Alessa, and she seemed to understand the situation, allowing them to bond on another level as military spouses.

"Are you happy about it?"

D's question cut through her thoughts and sent anger rushing through her. Even if things didn't work out between her and Jeffrey, this pregnancy was a wonderful thing. "Wow. D, if you want a place to stay until you figure things out, I suggest we close this topic because I can't handle another comment like that and still be able to bite my tongue."

"Hey, sis, I'm sorry. It's just…" As if she thought better of it, her words trailed off before she leaned back against the sofa and smiled. "I'm going to be an aunt."

"Aunt Dakota, now that's a scary thought." She relaxed in the recliner. "I know things with me and Jeffrey have been iffy at times, but things are going to change." *I hope so, at least.*

"You've told me that before."

Maybe so, but she had hope she didn't have before. The sparkle in Jeffrey's eyes when they spoke of their child was something that had been missing from him for a while. She only hoped that it would still be there when he returned from his deployment. Even though it was too early for her to be showing yet, she placed her hand on her stomach. *Your daddy fights for his country and has witnessed too much. Now we've got to show him there's more to life. We've got to fight for him. We can do that, right, baby girl?*

Girl? When had she decided it was going to be a girl? Or was that Jeffrey's earlier comment influencing her? She always thought he'd want a son first, and then maybe if they were lucky, a daughter. A son to teach how to throw a football, hit a baseball, and all of those other father-son moments. Yet, he seemed excited about the possibility of having a daughter.

When the doorbell rang again, Wyoming hopped off the chair and opened it, expecting it to be Alessa. Instead a delivery man stood on her porch, holding a package. "Mrs. Dorset?"

"Yes." Her eyebrow rose in question. Who was sending her something?

"Please sign here." He held out a clipboard and pen. After she signed her name, he handed her the box, bent down to retrieve another package in a decorative bag that she hadn't noticed, and held it out to her as well. "Have a great day."

"Umm…you too. Thanks." She stood there for a moment, holding the items and examining the labels.

"What's all that?" D rose off the sofa and came to stand next to Wyoming.

"Your guess is as good as mine." Wyoming noticed a small envelope on top of the box and slipped her finger under it to pull out a small card. *I already miss you. Jeffrey.* Tears sprang from her eyes and rolled freely down her cheeks.

"See, things are going to be different." She stepped back into the house, kicked the door shut, and went back to the recliner to open the packages. When she opened the small white box first, another notecard with Jeffrey's handwriting on it tumbled out. *Wear these and think of me.* Three tiny hearts were sketched below his words. Lifting the card, she found a pair of earrings, with three dangling hearts, connected in a row. *Our hearts. His, mine, and our child's.* Maybe it wasn't his thought when he'd purchased them, but it was hers now.

"For our daughter? You know it's going to be a girl?" D held the card that must have been attached to the second package and stared at Wyoming.

"Not yet, but he believes it's going to be a girl." Before her sister could question it further, she added, "Don't ask. It's an old family story." She set the box aside and leaned forward toward the decorative bag.

"Whatever it is, it's bigger than the baby will be."

With a light chuckle, she noticed D was right and untied the ribbon holding the bag closed. The plastic slipped down, revealing a large, stuffed elephant. The stuffed animal had to be almost twenty inches tall and fifteen wide, but the soft velvety gray material was adorable. She ran her hands over the elephant, caressing the long trunk and big ears. The soft pink bow around its neck matched the pink on the bottoms of the elephant's feet.

"You'd better have a girl now."

Wyoming didn't bother replying to D's comment. Instead, she leaned back in the recliner and cuddled the elephant to her chest. *He's thinking of us.* The very idea brought tears to her eyes again and hope rushed through her. Things were going to be different.

Chapter Four

Two days after the packages arrived, Wyoming sat at the kitchen table trying to work, but her thoughts kept returning to the family dinner planned for that evening. Telling their parents would have been less stressful with Jeffrey by her side, but she couldn't wait for him. This had to be done, and damned if she would let them spoil her mood. Dakota's reaction gave her an insight as to how their parents might react. At least Alessa had been happy for her. There was someone in her life who was excited and supportive. Even D had come around, but Wyoming didn't have hope that her mother would be supportive.

The computer in front of her buzzed, alerting her to an email, and the dread bubble around her popped as she clicked the alert to find the message was from Jeffrey. It was unbelievable that it had only been two days since she last saw him. This deployment seemed to be going slower than previous ones, and there was still too long until he'd be back home. She wanted him back home now. When he left, she wasn't sure that they would be able to make it work, but she was willing to give it a chance. Now she had a new hope that things would work out. Their son or daughter gave her hope that she might not have had otherwise. Putting the thoughts of their remaining time apart behind her, she clicked to open the email.

Stop worrying, baby. Tonight will go fine. Our parents…what can I say, other than they are who they are. Don't let them spoil our happiness. Bringing a child into this world is an amazing thing. Even though it's still hard to believe that we're going to be parents, I have no doubt we're going to be better ones than ours.

Ellie the elephant, as you've already named our daughter's stuffed animal, isn't too big. It's the perfect size for our little girl to grow into. It's also the first item for the nursery. Speaking of the nursery, when you're ready, Diamond and some of the guys will come over and move the furniture out. I'll be home before the crib is needed, so just leave it. I don't want you doing too much.

I've got to go. Are you wearing the earrings? Love you.

She was touched by his words. *Our happiness.* His happiness made her optimistic, though his reaction was unexpected. She hadn't anticipated his excitement over the pregnancy, even bracing herself for him to be upset about it.

She ran her finger lightly over the earrings that dangled from her ears, while using her free hand to hit reply. Since the arrival of the packages, she'd been wearing the earrings—except in bed. Crazy as it sounded, it made her feel closer to him. They were a small gift before he shipped out, but the meaning behind them touched her deeply.

Wearing them and missing you. D is here with me, so she'll help keep my parents in line. Your parents…well, let's just hope for the best. I wish you were here to tell them with me. Hopefully they'll be happy for us and accept they'll be grandparents in a few months.

I'm not worried about the nursery, but thanks for asking Diamond. Is it too early to start shopping for baby clothes at Heart of Diamond? Just kidding. You might believe we're having a girl, but I'd rather the doctor to confirm that before I go crazy on the nursery. I know you're never wrong, but let's just wait, shall we?

She smirked to herself. She could picture him standing before her, the cocky grin on his face. Rarely was he wrong, but it happened to even the best of them. Jeffrey didn't say something unless he was positive of the answer and he had no problem admitting it if he didn't know for certain. She rubbed her hand over her stomach. "You'll be a little girl just to get on your daddy's good side and prove once again he's always right. Won't you?"

D had another blowout with my parents, so she's staying here for a few days. It's been nice to have her around. I've been thinking about the basement apartment again. It's been empty since we bought the place. I know you don't want someone you don't know living there while you're deployed, but a fresh coat of paint and a little elbow grease is all it needs. Give it some thought when you have time. The extra income could be nice once the baby is here. There's so much that needs to be done before our...damn you, you almost had me saying 'our daughter's arrival.'

Needing to get back to work, she wrapped up the email, but before she hit send she grabbed her cell phone, snapped a picture so he could see she was wearing the earrings and attached it. As the email sent, she thought back to the last deployment. Even though it was over a year ago, she could still remember the email that marked the difference in him. She brushed it off, thinking it was the events weighing on him, and the unknown status of PFC Kyle Phillips. Only, it never got better, the distance between them growing.

Needing a boost, she shot Alessa a text, inquiring about what happened to Kyle. She didn't know the young Marine very well, but what happened to him could have happened to any of them. If Kyle hadn't been assigned to Diamond's squad, would Jeffrey have been in the Humvee that exploded when it ran over an IED? Would it have been her husband who came home injured? Or worse yet, would he have taken Weber's place? She'd rather have him back injured, than have to bury him like Cassy had to bury her husband.

Thinking about all of the horrible things that could happen to Jeffrey while he was overseas wouldn't make this deployment easier. *This isn't his first deployment. He'll be home safely soon.* Even as she reminded herself of this, she couldn't shake the dread settling over her. The knowledge that something could happen to him or any one of the Marines was a weight they all carried

29

with them. They just tried not to acknowledge it. As if not thinking about it could prevent it from happening. That the men in uniform would never show up at her door to deliver the worst news of her life.

"You seem lost in thought." D sank into the chair across from her. "Everything okay?"

"Yeah." She forced herself to give her sister a smile, even if it was the last thing she felt like doing. "You heading out? Don't forget that Mom and Dad will be here at six."

"I was going to go for a run, but if you're not working why don't we take a drive? In the paper this morning there was an advertisement for an apartment. It's only a couple miles away, and I thought I'd swing by and check it out."

"Sure." Wyoming clicked save on the document that was up and closed her laptop. "Work can wait. After all, what's the point of working from home and making your own hours if you can't take a little time off to spend with your sister? Let me grab my purse and I'm ready." She rose from the kitchen table and strolled back to her bedroom where her bag was, without saying a word about the basement apartment. If Jeffrey got her hints from the email, maybe D could move in downstairs. It was cute and cozy, and it would give D the opportunity to get away from their parents and out on her own without the struggles that Wyoming had before she met Jeffrey.

A few moments later, she returned, her purse slung over her shoulder. "How about we grab lunch while we're out? My treat."

"Marqui's Barbeque?" D shot off the chair and grabbed her bag. "Let's eat first. Barbeque and pickles."

"Makes me wonder who's pregnant." She teased and pulled open the door just as her mother, Dorothy, stormed up on the porch. "You're early. Everything okay?"

"Don't give me that shit!" Her mother stalked toward her, her eyes wide and her fists clenched, forcing her way inside. "How dare you embarrass me this way?"

"Mom? What happened?" D came up next to Wyoming as she shut the door.

"Stay out of this," Dorothy snapped without even looking at D, instead focusing on Wyoming. "Why the hell didn't you tell me you're pregnant? Instead I had to learn it from that blabbermouth Mary Tibbs. Do you know how embarrassed I was when she told me? What kind of daughter doesn't even tell her mother that she's pregnant? And what were you thinking?"

"That's why I invited you and Dad to dinner tonight. I wanted to tell everyone at the same time. Mr. and Mrs. Dorset will be here, too." She didn't know how Mrs. Tibbs found out, but at the moment it didn't matter as much as calming her mother down.

"What were you thinking, getting pregnant when you can't even get your husband to pay attention to you? I've seen the look in his eyes. He's not right in the head. He needs help. Whatever happened to him, he's not the same man as before. Why would you even consider bringing a child into *this* home?"

This home? How dare she spit out those two words as if there was something wrong with them? Her mother didn't know half the situation between her and Jeffrey. Whenever they had a family get-together, they put on an act, as thought everything was perfect between them. She might have told D about some of the strain between them, but never her mother. She wouldn't have understood and the last thing Wyoming wanted was the condescending remarks that her mother was famous for.

"Mom, you never approved of Jeffrey. You thought he wasn't good enough for your family and it never mattered that I love him."

"You're damn right I never liked him. What kind of husband can he be when he's gone as much as he is? Even when he's here physically, he's not here mentally. Not anymore. You need a husband like I found with your father. Not—"

"What's that, Mom? Someone you can push around? Someone who has a temper as much as you do?" She shook her head. "No, Mom. I don't want a house filled with fighting like it was when I was a kid. I want a happy home, one filled with love. I don't want my children to live in fear of saying the wrong thing that might bring on another fight. Don't you realize that's why I moved out on my eighteenth birthday? That's why D left, too. Neither of us could stand living like that."

"Is that how you feel?" Dorothy glanced over at D. "You too?"

"Mom, it's not healthy," D said, but Dorothy shook her head, cutting her off before she could continue.

"Very well. Your father and I are leaving on Monday to see his sister. I want your stuff out of our house before we return on Thursday." Dorothy turned and grabbed the door handle before glancing back at them again. "If that's how you both feel about your parents, I suggest we go our separate ways. You both obviously have your lives completely mapped out, and you don't need us."

"Mom—" Wyoming hollered, but her mother had already left, slamming the door behind her. How could she just cut off her children like that? The very idea was unbelievable for her, especially now that she was pregnant. The very idea of distancing herself from her child broke her heart. Wyoming and D had always had their differences with their parents, but the idea of going their separate ways was like a knife in her back. They would be grandparents in a few months and they wanted nothing to do with her, D, or their future grandchild. Even as she tried to hold back, she couldn't stop the tears from welling in her eyes. There was no blinking them away this time.

# Chapter Five

The afternoon of sister bonding time didn't go as well as Wyoming had hoped. It would have been nice for their time together to shake the bad mood, but things only got worse after they left the house. Marqui's Barbeque was closed because of a waterline break and the apartment they went to check out was horrible. Maybe the apartment not working out wasn't such a bad thing, because she wasn't looking forward to D leaving and the house being empty again.

"You know Mom, she'll come around." D leaned against the counter, knife in hand as she chopped the vegetables for the salad.

"I don't know." After checking the lasagna, she placed it back in the oven, shut the door, and turned back to her sister. "Maybe I don't want her to come around. All our lives, we've walked on eggshells because of her moods, doing whatever we could so we wouldn't cause another fight between our parents. I'm tired of it and it's not something I want for my child. I guess I'm realizing that I would rather not have the baby's grandparents in our lives if it means they have to deal with the same things we did."

"Mom never meant any harm, she's just…"

"Unstable?" Wyoming offered when her sister stumbled over the last part.

"No. Well, maybe, but I was going to use a different word." D tossed the cucumbers onto the salad and sat the knife aside. "When she stays on her medication, her moods are more balanced and the fighting is minimal."

"The problem is she won't stay on it. She doesn't like how it makes her feel and she refuses to try any other medications. Who ends up suffering? Dad and us. Not that Dad is innocent in all of this, either, but he's better."

"He does the complete opposite from what we do. Instead of doing whatever he can not to piss her off, he presses her buttons until she's boiling for a fight." D shook her head. "How did we ever end up normal with parents like them?"

"We stuck together and we spent as little time at home as possible. We didn't turn out too bad compared to what we came from, did we?" She grabbed the loaf of French bread that she'd bought while they were out and placed it on the cutting board.

"No, we didn't." D leaned against the counter for a long moment before the corners of her lips curled into a smile. "You know I haven't seen you this happy in a long time. I'm not sure if it's the pregnancy or because things are changing with you and Jeffrey, but either way, I'm delighted for you. Now, why don't you go get ready, take a few minutes to yourself, and I can handle the garlic bread."

"Thanks." She placed the knife next to the cutting board and stepped back. "If you want to make yourself scarce while the Dorsets are here, I understand. I roped you into this dinner when Mom and Dad were coming, but after earlier…"

"Not a chance. You might need my help when they ask where Mom is. I remember the last family dinner. Judy is sweet, but you know she's going to wonder where Mom and Dad are. Peter, on the other hand, is great. He always makes me laugh. Now go get ready, they'll be here soon."

"Thanks, D." Without further encouragement, she hurried down the hallway toward the master bedroom. Hopes of a peaceful dinner with her in-laws hurried her movements. Without her mother there to make uncomfortable comments, maybe her announcement would go smoother. Judy and Peter were like second parents to her, making her feel like a part of their family. They were the parents she always wished she had.

Jeffrey and Peter had their differences, most of it stemming from his father missing the majority of his childhood. Peter was career military, and deployments had played havoc throughout Jeffrey's youth. Jeffrey had wanted his father to come to his football and basketball games, but too often his duty had interfered. It wasn't until he was older that he realized his attitude was selfish, but by then it was too late. She encouraged him to fix the situation between him and his father, but whenever she brought it up he told her, "I don't know how to fix it. There's too much water under the bridge now."

Stepping into their room, she wondered if they could change things just as she was beginning to change things with him. "Maybe you can help bring them closer together. You can force your daddy and granddad to work things out." She could almost picture their little girl with both her dad and grandfather wrapped around her little finger. *There I go again, thinking I'm having a girl.* Even as she scolded herself for thinking that way, she couldn't help but be excited at the possibility.

Without any time to spare, she hurried to change and touch up her makeup before her in-laws' arrival. The last thing she wanted to do was leave D alone with them when she was doing her a favor by sticking around, even without their parents' presence.

Setting her eyeliner pencil aside, she leaned closer to the mirror and took in her appearance. There in the mirror, her father's eyes shined back at her, so full of suspicion and a darkness that she knew lingered within her. The tiny bump in her nose made it seem as though her nose was broken at one time, but it hadn't been. Instead it had been a gift from her mother's side. Would these features be passed on to her child? She hoped their child would take after Jeffrey's natural good looks, but at the very least, she hoped they wouldn't have the same doubt hidden within their eyes as she did.

"They won't because they won't witness the same shit D and I did." She snatched the pencil off the bathroom counter, determined to make her eyes look different. The darkness might be within her, but the world didn't need to see it whenever they looked at her. "The dark cloud hanging overhead that won't go away…that's what I am. How did Jeffrey ever fall in love with me when I'm such a pessimist?"

The doorbell rang, echoing through the house, and a moment later D's voice carried down the hallway. "Take your time. I'll get it."

Tossing her eyeliner pencil into her makeup bag, she stepped back and let out a sigh. "Here goes nothing. Hopefully they take it better than Mom did." Even with her nervousness about how the Dorsets would handle the news, she knew they'd take it better than her own mother did. Mr. and Mrs. Dorset were a normal family, at least compared to what she had to judge them against. They'd welcome the new addition to their family just as they welcomed her.

"It's so good to see you again." Judy's voice was almost musical as she wrapped her arms around D as if she was another daughter.

"You too, Mrs. Dorset."

"Now none of that Mrs. Dorset stuff." Judy had been adamant that they call her by her first name, or Mom.

Five years ago when Wyoming joined the family, she had been reserved when it came to calling Judy Mom, fearful she would be too much like her own mother. Now it was nice to have someone down to earth and sane to consider a mother, even if it was only through marriage. Soon she'd be a grandmother and at least their child would have one sane grandmother in her life. For the first time since she found out she was pregnant, excitement bubbled within her and she wasn't sure if she could make it until dessert to make the announcement, like she planned.

"Mom…" Wyoming stepped out of the hallway from where she had paused, watching the two of them. "I'm so glad you could make it."

"We're a little early, but you know Peter, he hates to be late."

"You're always welcome here. Where is he?" Expecting him to stroll into the house at any moment, she glanced toward the door.

"Business call." Judy shook her head as she hugged Wyoming. "Why I ever got him involved in flipping houses, I'll never know. This latest house has been one problem after another and his contractor called as we were pulling in. I don't know what it was about, but Peter didn't look happy."

She returned the hug and allowed the feeling of comfort she found in their embrace to wash over her and calm her. "I know you love to see the houses go from the state you purchase them in, to the dream house that someone will raise a family in. I've seen the work you and Dad put into those houses and it's nothing short of spectacular. You nag at him for working too much, but you work just as hard. You might not realize it, but every time we've gone shopping together, I see you looking at things you can use. You specialize in the design features and because you enjoy that, it doesn't seem like work to you."

"You're one to talk. Everyone who checks out our website wants to know who created it. You've worked your magic to showcase the houses and what we're doing."

"That's why my business took off like it has. The best form of promotion is word of mouth." She extended her arm out to the living room behind them. "Let's sit. Dinner's not quite ready yet."

"Too busy for another client?" Judy asked as she took a seat on the sofa.

"Depends on who, the project, and the timeframe." Wanting to feel closer to Jeffrey, Wyoming sat in his recliner as her sister moved to the remaining chair. "You know I always make time for you and your friends."

"Actually it's not a friend of mine, but a Marine that Jeffrey served with, Kyle Phillips. Him and his wife, Staci, bought a ranch and are now operating United Homefront Ranch for service members. They focus on helping veterans adjust to civilian life, and those who are suffering with PTSD. The one-time horse ranch is becoming a safe place for those who risked so much for us. Now he's looking to create a web presence so that others can find him, and naturally I thought of you."

"I read an article about him recently. He's come so far since…" D's words trailed off as she glanced over at her sister. "I'm sorry."

Memories of that day washed over her and she could almost picture herself standing on the porch with D as the dark sedan pulled onto the block. For a moment she thought her worst nightmares had happened and they were coming to her door to tell her Jeffrey wouldn't be coming home. But it wasn't her door, it was Cassy Weber who lived directly across the street. Weber served with Jeffrey's unit, and they were deployed together. Everyone knew something happened to their unit, but Weber's death hadn't been what she expected. Cassy was now a widow with a young son. In the weeks following her husband's death, Wyoming watched as the woman tried to hold it together for her son's sake. Their lives would never be the same.

Cassy hightailed it out of Virginia, and rushed back to her hometown where they'd bury Weber. She couldn't handle being surrounded by the military any longer. Now living across the country, she was turning things around and made Weber's death mean something. She built her business Sewn With Love, in memory of her husband, turning the uniforms and clothes of fallen service members into something special for their spouses and families. It began as a way to remember those who were killed in action, but it had gone far beyond that. Any spouse or family member could send in clothes and she would turn them into whatever they wanted. Quilts were the most popular, but she also made pillows, purses, and more. The newspaper article Wyoming read about Cassy's business flashed in her mind: *Cassy Weber has done something for his memory, and for the memories of others who died during their service to our country. She's turning tragedy into something that's cherished. She gave her husband's life and his death meaning, and by doing that, she's giving others closure.*

It could have easily been Jeffrey that day. She was forever thankful he made it home to her, even if he was a slightly different man now. She placed her hand on her stomach, gently rubbing over the spot where their baby was growing. *We're going to make that change. We're going to help him see there's still good in the world, and that it's okay to be happy.*

Chapter Six

Seated at the head of the table, Wyoming reached up to caress her earrings, reminding herself that even though Jeffrey was missing this moment, he would be back for the birth of their child and that was what really mattered. This wasn't the first time he hadn't been there and it wouldn't be the last. When she married a Marine, she knew he'd be away occasionally and there would be holidays, birthdays, and other special occasions he'd miss. Because of that, she always planned to cherish the moments he was there.

"Dinner was delicious." Judy placed her napkin on the table next to her plate. "With all your spare time, you should bottle your pasta sauce. It's better than anything on the market."

"My spare time will soon be more limited."

"Oh, Wyoming, if this is because of the job—"

"Mom. This isn't about the job for Kyle. I'm more than happy to do that, and I'm looking forward to that project." Wyoming pushed back from the table. "I'm pregnant."

"Oh, Wyoming." Tears leaked from Judy's eyes as she pulled back from the table. "Jeffrey…does he know?"

With a nod, she let out the breath she had been holding. For a brief moment, she almost thought Judy was going to ask if it was his child, and just the thought that her mother-in-law would ask that tightened her chest. "The doctor called confirming what I thought the morning he left and I told him before he left. He thinks it's going to be a girl."

"Our family wives' tale." Peter shook his head. "It's true, but Jeffrey has always done things his own way. I wouldn't be one bit surprised if you end up giving him a son instead."

"This is wonderful news." Judy rose from her chair and came over to her. "We're going to be grandparents. Something I wasn't sure would ever happen."

"Why?" she asked as Judy embraced her.

"I didn't even know you two were thinking about starting a family," Judy said quickly without looking at her.

"Don't lie to her. She deserves the truth." Peter shook his head. "Jeffrey always resented my military career because it took me away from him. He saw every missed football or baseball game as a direct hit against him. He asked me once if he was a better son, would I be there for his games like all of the other fathers."

"It wasn't only that, but Jeffrey has been so distant since the last deployment." Judy stepped back toward her husband, placed her hand on his shoulder, and he reached up to lay his hand over hers. "Even though neither of you said anything, I could see the distance between you. Over the years, every military spouse goes through it. We did. A marriage with one of the spouses in the military has challenges that others don't, but if they love each other enough to fight for their marriage like they'll fight for their country, they'll get through it. I had hope you and Jeffrey would get through it."

She didn't know what to say. Things were still rocky between them, but for the first time she could feel Jeffrey trying. Would it continue? She wasn't sure. But not just for the sake of their child, but for the sake of their marriage, she was willing to fight for him. She loved him and she knew he loved her.

The distance he put between them wasn't because of her or a lack of love between them. He would see the walls he built, keeping her out, as a way of protecting her. She didn't want to be protected or sheltered from him.

"I shouldn't have said anything." Judy took a step closer to her, but paused as if she didn't know what to do.

"It's fine. Like every marriage, we've had our problems but we're getting through them. Things are working out and he's ecstatic about the pregnancy. We both are." She looked up at her in-laws and smiled. "He's going to make a great dad."

"And I'm going to be the kid's favorite aunt." D returned to the table with the cake in hand. "Which is why we're going to celebrate right now with chocolate cake, because it's Wyoming's favorite."

"Did you miss that you're their only aunt?" Wyoming let out a light chuckle and shook her head. "We're a small family but we're close, and that's what I want for my little girl...or boy."

"What about your parents? Have you told them? I thought they'd be here today."

"Something came up." D answered before Wyoming could.

"They know." Wyoming nodded. "Let's have cake. I've been eyeing it since D baked it this afternoon." Anything so they wouldn't have to talk about her parents. She was still a rollercoaster of emotions when it came to the whole situation. How dare her mother blame her? But more to the point, why did the reaction even surprise her? Her mother had always been like that.

The rest of the evening was spent talking about the baby and reminiscing about Jeffrey's childhood. His face would have burned red with mortification at the stories his parents shared. If they had known what the night's news would have been, she didn't doubt they would have brought their many photo albums of embarrassing baby pictures. While she was sure that would have been something to remember, she was also relieved on his behalf.

There were things about her childhood that she never wanted him to learn. If her parents had cared more about her and D while they were growing up instead of themselves, maybe there would be uncomfortable stories and horrifying pictures for him to see as well. Instead they had their hospital birth pictures and a scarce few others from their whole lives. Her parents, on the other hand, had pictures from their trips around the world while the girls were stuck with their grandparents.

Someone once told her that if you wanted to see what someone was afraid of losing, see what they took pictures of. If that was true, did it prove how little her parents valued their own children? No, they'd shown that with their actions. She never wanted her children to have the same doubts that she had about her parents. Her children would know she loved them and they'd have a home filled with love. Even if things don't work out with Jeffrey, she knew he'd be in their child's life. *Things are going to work out and our baby will have both parents in the same house filled with love. She'll have grandparents and an aunt that will spoil her rotten. Our baby will never question whether she was wanted or loved, because we'll show her every day that she is.*

Chapter Seven

Days passed before Wyoming received another email from Jeffrey. It wasn't unusual, as communication and Internet access could be sketchy at times. The delayed response might have landed in her inbox at the perfect time. She woke up an emotional wreck and a message from him was just what she needed to lighten the mood.

I can't believe my mother told you those stories. I was an innocent child and she's making it up. I cannot believe her. I miss a family dinner and she tells you something she promised me she'd never tell a living person. Okay, I'm over my shock. Tell me D left the room before Mom started the story about me walking through the school buck naked? Otherwise, I'll never be able to face her. She'll rag me about it forever.

Mom conveniently left out that I was sick and dying. That was the worst flu of my life. But did she mention any of that? No. She just told you that I stripped out of my clothes while the nurse thought I was resting until my mother came to pick me up. I was hot from the fever and the cafeteria was always cold. That's where I was going. My timing could have been better and I could have waited until everyone returned to their classrooms from recess but, no, not me. I wanted to show the world my naked body.

Mom always got a kick out of that story, but thankfully our neighbor, Mrs. Knight, was a kindergarten teacher at the school. She spotted me and whisked me away before I could impress the girls in my class. Even as I fought her she tugged off her sweater, wrapped it around me and picked me up to take me back to the nurse's office. Mom arrived while all this was going on and was yelling at the nurse because she lost me when Mrs. Knight carried me back into the office. Mom was furious with the nurse for what happened and ranted about how I could have walked out of the school without anyone noticing. You know Mom, she's always been a worrier.

Do me a favor, if our children ever have embarrassing stories like this, don't tell anyone. It will scar our child for life. Also tell Mom she's not allowed to tell any more embarrassing stories about me.

I'm sorry about your parents. Have you heard from them yet? Your mom might take a bit of time, but you know she'll cool off and come around. She's upset because she wasn't the first to know. Maybe your dad could talk to her? Remember how upset she was when we got married? But she came around. Maybe it was more D than your dad who helped bring her around, but the idea of a grandchild would be enough for her to forget about this petty issue. If she wants to be a part of our child's life, she's going to have to forgive you. Not that you did anything wrong and where she gets off being angry is beyond me. I'd suggest D trying to talk to her, but since she's having her own problems with your parents, I don't think that's going to help anything.

I don't mind D staying there, but long-term isn't going to work. The guest room is going to be turned into the nursery and you need to keep your office. Kicking her out isn't my style either. She's family. If you think you two are up for it, then clean up the basement apartment, and let her stay there. She'll be away from your folks and close by for our little girl. It will also give her a place to stay, where she's on her own but not alone. Charging her rent isn't necessary. Let her use that money for college.

This arrangement would work for a few months at least. My contract ends in nine months and decision time is coming. I had planned on reenlisting, but with the baby...I want to be home more. I don't want to miss all of the things my dad missed when I was growing up. I want to be there when our little girl takes her first steps and says her first word. I want to be home with you and prove to you that I still want you. Maybe even convince you to give me a few more daughters and a son or two. We talked about having a

48

large family…let's make it happen. I'm not sure what I'll do yet, but I want to be there with my girls.

The rest of his email was a blur. He wanted to leave the military to spend more time with her and the baby. This announcement took her by surprise. It was so unexpected and heartwarming that she had to read it twice more before it sank in. It was a complete change from when they'd discussed marriage. Shortly after he proposed, he told her that he was career military and didn't see himself leaving until he was too old to keep up with the younger men. Military life, deployments, and risks were supposed to be with her for years to come, but now it was changing.

Was she happy about it? Hell yes. The idea of him wanting to make that change so he would be there with her and their child was enough to bring tears to her eyes. When she found out she was pregnant, the thought of him leaving the Marines never crossed her mind. This was his career and he loved what he did. She never thought he put his career in front of her, but for the first time he showed that her and the baby were more important to him than anything else.

This change was unforeseen, but she wondered if he hadn't considered it before. The papers for his reenlistment came weeks before and he hadn't signed them. Had the last deployment been weighing on his thoughts enough to make him consider leaving the Marines? Maybe he realized how close he had come to being injured or killed. But she couldn't see Jeffrey leaving because of that. He was a man who would rather be there and be in the action than back home on the sidelines. He'd rather be there to help his brothers-in-arms. However, this pregnancy had given him a new insight on what was important.

Life changed all around her. While it felt a little nerve-wracking because she didn't know what to expect, she was also excited. When he returned, they'd have a whole new future to look forward to together. One that included them being parents.

Chapter Eight

The deployment was going faster than any of the previous ones for Wyoming. Weeks flew by in the blink of an eye and they were already halfway through. Her pregnancy went smoothly, as well, even though her cravings were out of control. Twenty-two weeks in, and finally their child decided to cooperate enough for them to learn the sex. The first time they tried, the baby was in the wrong position. Now she knew and she couldn't believe it.

"Stop staring at the sonogram picture." D shook her head as she handed Wyoming her laptop. "Email Jeffrey and let him know."

"A girl…"

"I know. I'm going to have a niece." D dropped onto the sofa. "And a nephew."

"Twins." Wyoming was still accepting the news herself. "I can't believe we didn't know before."

"Your little girl was hogging the spotlight, keeping her brother hidden." D leaned back against the sofa and pulled her legs up under her. "I guess that throws a little dirt on to Jeffrey's theory that it would be a girl because of the month you conceived in."

"A little." She opened her laptop, hit the power button, and watched it come to life. The shock was wearing off, only to be replaced with anxiety.

She had begun to prepare for the baby, but she hadn't considered twins. There was so much that would need to be done. She'd have to purchase two of everything and start from scratch on the nursery plans. Figuring Jeffrey was right, she'd been considering painting the walls pink, but with a boy she'd need to go with a more neutral color and add colors with their bedding and decorations. "At least I'll never have to worry about telling them apart. If they were identical twins, I could just see Jeffrey calling them by their wrong names."

"You both wanted a big family and now you're on the road to it. Does his side have multiples?"

"I don't know." Her cell phone rang. She expected it to be Judy calling to find out how the appointment went, and she quickly added before answering, "Guess we're about to find out."

"She's going to be over the moon."

Wyoming shook her head and didn't bother to look at the caller ID as she brought the phone to her ear. "Hello, Judy."

"Well, that's a name I haven't been called before." Jeffrey's voice filled the line, sending her heart fluttering in her chest.

"Jeffrey…"

"Yeah, baby." His words soothed her, comforting her from afar. "We're about to move out, so I don't have long, but I wanted to find out how the appointment went. Are we having a little girl?"

"Yes—"

A holler of excitement came through the line. "A daughter. I told you! I can't believe it."

"You were only half right."

"Huh?" Confusion filled his voice.

"Twins…a girl and a boy. Your son was hidden behind his sister. That's how we missed it."

"Twins." He repeated it.

"Yes."

"No fucking way! I can't believe it. Are you okay?"

"We're fine." She placed her hand on her ever-growing stomach. "We just got back from the doctor's office and I was about to email you a picture of the sonogram. Our babies are both healthy and I'm feeling pretty good. D is taking good care of me, even went out last night to get me ice cream."

"Dorset. Let's go, we're moving out," a voice said in the background.

"Baby, I've got to go. Email me that picture and take care of our babies."

"Be safe. I love you." She glanced down at the clock on her laptop and tried not to think about the late hour. Darkness might help give them extra coverage, but it also made it harder for them to spot the dangers surrounding them. *He'll be okay and he'll be home soon.* This was his last deployment. The paperwork to leave the Marines had already been filed and processed. He'd be a civilian again before she knew it.

"It's more important now than it was before," he added. "Talk to D about what I said in the email. I love you and I'll be home soon."

Before she could reply, the line went dead, leaving her with a mixture of emotions. Not wanting to deal with the work she had planned on doing, she shut her laptop and set it aside on the end table. He was right; twins would mean more work and she needed to decide what she wanted to do with her business. She liked his idea, but she was concerned it could cause a divide between her and D. After already losing her parents, she wasn't sure she wanted to distance herself from the last family member she had.

"You okay?"

She glanced up to see D with her eyebrow cocked in question, as she watched her intently. "I…"

"Oh no, what's wrong? You're not going to fall to pieces on me, are you?" D scooted down the sofa toward the chair Wyoming was sitting on.

"Do you want some ice cream? I'll get you some. Whatever you want, just name it."

"I'm fine." She grinned at her sister. "Having twins changes things. I have jobs lined up months in advance and scaling back like I planned isn't going to work when you consider twins. A baby is a lot of work, twins even more so."

"What are you saying?"

"I never asked you to work with me full-time because I'm a control freak and I'd be a demanding boss. We're not only sisters but we're best friends and the idea of causing a conflict between us because of work didn't sit well with me." She ran her hand over her stomach, trying to soothe the babies within as they kicked and fluttered. "You know my work inside and out and I've freelanced stuff to you in the past, so I know you can handle it. I'd like for you to consider leaving your current position to work for me full-time. You can handle the jobs I have scheduled and once I'm back to being able to work, we'll be able to take on double the jobs. Considering how much Judy promotes the business, I have no doubt that will fill quickly. I already have a waitlist as long as my arm."

"I know you considered going to college but you could put that on hold until next year. If this is what you want to do, you don't need to go to school for it. I've gone the degree route and I didn't learn anything in college that I didn't already know. It was a waste of money, but at that time I thought I'd end up working for someone. I started doing some freelance work just to pass the time while Jeffrey was deployed."

"That's when you did the website for Judy and Peter," D added.

"Yes and my world opened up. My business took off practically overnight and now I have more work than I can handle."

"Your office isn't big enough for both of us to work out of it and you just turned the basement apartment into living quarters for me. Maybe we

54

should have swapped that. I mean, if I'm going to work here with you, then we're going to need more of a workspace. With some work, we could turn the basement living area into what we need."

"That's the other thing." Wyoming kicked off her shoes and adjusted in the recliner, making herself comfortable. "With Jeffrey leaving the Marines, there's no reason for us to stay here. This place is too small for twins. The workspace would be inadequate for me, let alone for the two of us if you take the position."

"You're moving?" D's jaw hung open slightly in surprise.

"Jeffrey received a job offer. With Peter, believe it or not. I knew nothing about it until two weeks ago when Jeffrey emailed me to discuss it."

"How? I mean, Peter offered Jeffrey a job? Doing what?"

"It's hard to believe." Wyoming chuckled. "Jeffrey worked with a family friend all through high school restoring houses, so he has experience. When Peter heard that Jeffrey wasn't reenlisting, he decided it was the perfect opportunity. They've had some issues in the past, but Peter wants to make things better between them. They also want to be part of their grandchildren's lives and with Mom and Dad being absent, these kids deserve to have that."

Giving D a moment to absorb the information, Wyoming grabbed the bottle of water from the coffee table in front of her and took a long swig. "There is a place a few miles from my in-laws that Peter is almost finished remolding. It's perfect. A large four-bedroom house with an artist's studio and a guest house. Jeffrey suggested we sell this place and move there. You can have the guest house and Peter assures him the studio is large enough that I can hire half a dozen workers and it won't be crowded. The kids will have a huge yard to play in and there's even an in-ground pool."

"Leave Virginia Beach…I don't know. What happens when the kids are old enough and you don't need me—"

"This isn't a temporary position. I want you to become my partner. There's no one else I'd rather be in business with, and I know you have the same dedication to this that I do." Wyoming scooted to the edge of the chair and slowly rose. "Just think about it. If you're not interested, I understand. When we move, we can work out something and you can stay here. I'm going to go take a hot bath. If Judy calls, tell her I'll call her back in a bit, and don't you dare tell her twins."

Without waiting, Wyoming headed down the hall toward the master bedroom and the Jacuzzi tub that was calling her name. She needed a little bit of time to herself and a hot soak in the tub seemed like the perfect idea. It would give her time to adjust to the news of having twins. More than anything, that revelation was the one that threw her off-kilter. A son and daughter at once. Was she ready for two babies? Not that it mattered; they'd be here in just a few months. Ready or not.

Chapter Nine

Six months flew by and now Wyoming stood in the airport baggage claim area waiting for Jeffrey's arrival. She was eight and a half months pregnant and her stomach was full and round from the twins. It was difficult to find a comfortable spot and each day had gotten worse. In the last week she was worried that Jeffrey wouldn't make it home before she went into labor. Now the day was here and in a few minutes' time she would see him strolling down the airport corridor. He had told her to stay home and rest, that D could pick him up, but she couldn't do that. She needed to be here to see him and welcome him home.

During this deployment, things changed between them. They grew closer through their email exchanges, reminiscing about the past, making plans for the future and their children, but most of all they fell in love all over again. In order to believe it, she needed to see him in person. That would confirm everything that had happened between them over the last few months. It would be the confirmation that the words typed in the emails exchanged weren't just fluff and that he meant everything he said.

A kick from her unborn children made her hand slide to her stomach. "Daddy's almost here." As she rubbed her stomach she knew that it was their little boy kicking. He was a fighter, just like his father. Their daughter preferred to aim her kicks at Mommy's ribs, as if needing to be different than her brother.

"Waiting for someone?" A rough voice came from behind her, instantly sending chills through her.

Even though the voice sounded deeper and there was a lightness to his words, she recognized it. How had he gotten past her? "Jeffrey?" She spun around to face him and found him standing there in his camouflage uniform. The distance and darkness she saw in his gaze before he'd left was gone, and now his smile sparkled in his eyes. His hair was a little longer and there was stubble along his jawline from traveling for most of the last two days, but he'd finally arrived.

He dropped his bag at his feet and wrapped his arms around her. "How's my beautiful wife? Taking good care of my babies, I hope."

"Oh, Jeffrey!" She wrapped her arms around his neck and pressed herself against him. The simple embrace was different this time because it wasn't just one-sided. He hugged her tight, his face pressed against her neck.

"Baby, I missed you." He placed a tender kissed along the curve of her neck before pulling back.

"How did you get past me? I've been here for the last fifteen minutes. I didn't see you come down the hall."

He pulled back enough to look at her but didn't end the embrace. "Last minute, I was bumped to an earlier fight and arrived forty minutes ago. I ran into an old boot camp buddy and we were talking, otherwise I'd have been down here when you arrived. Where's D?"

"She's circling the airport. I suggested we park so she could come in, but I think she was giving us a little time to ourselves." She brushed her hand along the side of his face and the stubble teased along the pads of her fingers.

"How is she working out with your business? Is she ready for when the kids are here?"

"She's perfect. She's handling most of the stuff herself already, but there are a couple projects I haven't been able to give up yet. Mom and Dad's mostly. My hands are still all over United Homefront Ranch, but she's at least assisting on the website design." She let out a light chuckle. "I think she's ready for me to take a break so she can prove herself, instead of having me checking things over her shoulders."

"Good. Because I want some time with just you. I want to prove to you that I'm a different man."

"You already have. Otherwise I wouldn't be moving away from Virginia Beach and starting over. But this will be good for us. It will be good for you and Dad, and our kids need their grandparents around. This is going to be good for all of us. We're going to make this work. I love you, Jeffrey."

"I love you, too." He tipped his head to the side and kissed the palm of her hand. "Let's get out of here and get you off your feet."

"Your parents put off arriving until the morning."

"I know." He grabbed his bag and slid it over his shoulder before slipping his arm around her so that his hand rested on the small of her back. "Dad emailed me to let me know. They wanted to give us time alone together before they came. He figured we had a lot of time to make up before the babies arrive. Twins…I still can't believe it."

"Me either, but Lucky and Ace have been a huge help with the furniture for the nursery. They both brought some of their guys with them so they had it all taken care of quickly. Mac and Nicole have twins, so we spent most of the time talking about the double duty we're about to have. Wynn and Gwen are amazing also."

"The SEAL guys stick together, so I'm not surprised they all showed up to help. I figured Lucky would just recruit some of the guys from the unit, not his brother and the entire SEAL team."

"Me too, but Lucky said who better than the guys who have kids already? They could put the stuff together and the women could do what they do best and chat."

"That's Lucky, all right." He laughed as he led her outside. "Gwen and Wynn are practically attached at the hips. They work together and they're best friends."

"They're family, and family sticks together. They work well together, just like D and I do. I've been to Heart of Diamond and saw it firsthand. They have pride in their work and I hope we can bring that to life with their website."

"Does that mean you've got another client?" He paused next to the curb and looked down at her.

"Yes." Grinning, she waved to D as she came into view so that she knew they were waiting. The SUV she traded her small car for when she found out she was having twins came to a stop right in front of them and a moment later D jumped out from behind the wheel.

"I'm so proud of you." He kissed the top of her head before D could come around the SUV to stand next to them.

"Welcome home! You ready to be a dad?" D wrapped her arms around him.

"More than ready. I hear you're stepping into your role as auntie already. Painting the nursery, shopping with Wyoming, and dealing with my parents. You deserve a medal."

"Because of you two, I have a job, a house, and I will soon have two little babies to love on, so no medal is needed."

"It's not just a job, it's a career, a business," Wyoming reminded her as Jeffrey tossed his bag into the back of the SUV.

"I know, but it doesn't feel like that. I never thought work was supposed to be fun. I get up every morning and look forward to getting started." D opened the passenger door.

"I hope it stays that way." With a hand on her stomach she moved to the passenger door and climbed into the seat. "Let's get home. I'm starving."

"Speaking of food, I made your reservations at Lynn's for six. There's no better way of celebrating Jeffrey's homecoming than an evening out for just the two of you." She tossed the keys to him. "You drive."

"I thought we'd have a quiet dinner at home," Wyoming said as D went to shut her door.

"Tomorrow. Judy and Peter will be here. Tonight needs to be about the two of you." She shut the door before Wyoming could argue further.

A night out with just her and Jeffrey. How long had it been since they did that? Too long. It had to be at least two years since they had a date night. Tonight, that would change. She'd wear the single black maternity dress she'd bought for the off chance she had to meet with a client and dress up more than she normally did. It would be a chance to start their new life together.

Chapter Ten

Dinner at Lynn's was amazing as always and what better way of reconnecting with each other than the place where they first met. Jeffrey slipped his arm along the curve of Wyoming's back as they strolled out of the restaurant and toward the beach. It was turning into a flawless evening and a perfect way for Jeffrey to celebrate being home. The idea of being a father in a few short weeks was still a little unnerving, but with Wyoming by his side he knew it was a battle he'd enjoy. The pregnancy had gone by in the blink of an eye and he was disappointed that he'd missed most of it. Next time, he'd be there every step of the way because the Marines would soon be a distant memory. They would start the next chapter of their lives soon enough.

"We're going to have to find another restaurant to celebrate at." Wyoming leaned down to pick up her heels that she'd kicked off and stepped onto the sandy beach.

"There's that little Italian place that we love by Mom's," He reminded her. "And we'll be back. We have friends and family here."

"Friends at least." She stared out at the ocean as they made their way down to the moonlit shore. "Our family is going to be with us."

"Your parents—"

"Want nothing to do with us, our kids, or D. Mom hasn't spoken to either of us since she stormed out, and Dad…" She leaned into his embrace and rested her head on his chest. "When D and I ran into him a couple months ago, he asked us to stop calling. He said that whenever there's a message from either of us, it only upsets Mom more and he's tired of her taking it out on him."

He stopped before they could reach the shore and pulled her around so she was in front of him. "It doesn't ease the loss, but I'm sorry. Your mom has always been…judgmental about your life, finding drama where there was none. You always said you hated growing up with all the fighting and attitude from her. Maybe this is for the best so that our children don't suffer through that as well."

"I know you're right. D and I talked about it and I even told her I'd rather them not be in our lives than constantly fight with them. I'm just an emotional mess. Let's blame it on pregnancy hormones. Just hold me."

He pulled her as close as he could with her stomach between them and wrapped his arms around her. "I love you, Wyoming, and I hate to see you upset because of them."

They stood there, embracing as the world passed them by, and the waves slammed against the shore. Nothing else mattered to them but that moment. He had her in his arms, right where she was meant to be.

"You should have seen her the day she came to the house screaming at me because someone else found out I was pregnant before I told her. She was livid and all because Mrs. Tibbs saw me looking at this crochet baby blanket at the craft show the day before my parents were coming for dinner. It was beautiful but I didn't know the sex, so I pocketed the card." She tipped her head up to look at him. "I could have been looking for a baby shower gift for a friend or anything, but you know Mrs. Tibbs."

"She's a busybody and loves to gossip."

"Maybe it was for the best. My mother wouldn't have been happy about the pregnancy, anyway. Learning the news from someone else allowed me to have a nice celebration with your parents and D. They were so happy about the news."

He rubbed his hand up her arm before reaching up to cup the side of her face. "Your mom never held back the fact she thought you deserved someone better than me as your husband. Her distaste for me seemed to grow over the last year or two. Which I can't blame her for. I haven't been the best man for you, but things will be different. I love you, Wyoming, and I don't want to lose you."

"I'm not going anywhere." She rose up on her toes and pressed her lips to his. "I love you and you're stuck with me."

"Good, because I have everything I want right here. You and our son and daughter are all I need." Without stepping back, he placed his hand on the side of her stomach and felt something he couldn't explain. "Is..."

"Your son is trying to say hello." She chuckled. "You should see your face. The shock has your eyes wide and your mouth slightly open. It's normal. Our daughter prefers to kick a little higher, near my ribs." She wrapped her hand around his wrist and gently pulled it up toward the curve of her stomach.

"What..."

"Just feel." She stopped moving his hand but didn't let go of his wrist. "Our babies are active."

"Wow." The gentle thump from his daughter was amazing. He was amazed by how she didn't seem bothered by any of it. There were two new lives growing within her. "Doesn't it hurt?"

"Not normally. Your son is a fighter, just like his daddy. He's got a harder kick than his sister. So it's good he's not up there by my ribs. They are active most of the time, and at first it was hard to get used to the sensation.

I'd wake up in the middle of the night wondering what happened and then they'd kick again."

"Dorset, is that you?" A man strolled toward them and it took him a moment to realize it was Lucky Diamond. There were two men and three women a little farther back, but they were in the shadows and he couldn't make them out.

"Gunnery Sergeant Diamond, what are you doing here?" He stepped back from her and wrapped his arm around her shoulders before offering a hand to Lucky.

"Family dinner." He tipped his head to his wife, Madison, his brother Ace with his wife Gwen, and his sister Wynn with her husband Jared "Boom" Taylor. Unlike Lucky, Ace and Boom were Navy SEALs. Even with the different career paths, the Diamond family was as tight-knit as any could be. "Why don't you join us? I know the ladies would love to catch up with Wyoming again."

"Not tonight. We already have plans. How about another time before we leave?"

"Leave?" Lucky raised an eyebrow. "I know you're leaving the Marines, but I hadn't heard you were moving out of the area."

"We're moving close to my parents. The kids will have their grandparents nearby and there'll be a huge lot to play in as they grow."

"The studio for my business is perfect," Wyoming added. "With D working for me now, we need a bigger space."

"I spoke to your sister this morning about my website." Wynn came to stand next to Lucky. "We were discussing the upcoming line and the ideas Gwen and I had about how to showcase some of it on the site. I was nervous about working so closely with someone else after all the time we've put into my two business websites, but talking with her today helped eliminate my concerns. She's talented and had some great ideas."

66

"I wouldn't have brought on someone I didn't have complete confidence in, but it's good to hear that. I've been a little clingy, not wanting to give up any of the work, but soon I won't have a choice." She ran her hand over her bulging stomach and smiled.

"I was the same way but it all works out. Somehow I've found the balance between my shops, designing, and my family. You will, too," Wynn reassured her.

"We better be going, it's almost seven." Boom slipped his hand into Wynn's. "You know that Lynn's doesn't like to hold late reservations."

"I'm having a cookout next weekend. Why don't you join us?" Ace suggested from a few steps behind Lucky and the others, his arm around his wife's waist. "Don't worry, it won't just be guys from my team, Lucky's invited some of your unit. It would be a great evening together before you head out."

"He's right, your last day is right around the corner," Lucky added. "Bring your sister, too. Wynn and Gwen can meet her in person to ease any hesitations they might have about someone else taking over."

"We have no hesitations now, but we'd still love to meet her," Gwen clarified from where she stood with Ace. "What do you say?"

"We'll be there." Jeffrey nodded. "Now, you'd better run along. Lynn will roast you alive if you're late. She hollered at us for being early."

"Then she saw my stomach and ushered us directly to a table. I'm going to miss her and the food."

After a few quick goodbyes and a hushed word between the women, they were alone again. She leaned back against him, staring out at the water again. He could tell she was lost in thought. Instead of asking her what was on her mind, he stood there enjoying the feeling of having her back in his arms. This was what he'd looked forward to and what got him through the days while he was overseas.

Her words before he left forced him to face his demons. He found a way to work through the darkness that plagued him since his last deployment. Every time he thought about giving up, he pictured her face and remembered that he was going to be a father. To say that he didn't still struggle with what happened and Weber's death was an understatement, but he refused to allow it to control him and steal his wife from him. Wyoming and his children were everything to him. They were what was important.

"I don't know what I'm going to miss more, them or the ocean."

"We'll be back," he assured her. "We're doing this for all of us. If you don't want to—"

She spun around to face him and her long brown hair billowed out around her. "No, I want to go. I love the house, my studio, and D loves the guest house. I know it's going to be perfect. You know me and change." She gave him an uneasy smile.

"I know, baby." He understood all too well what she meant. He had been in the Marines since he was eighteen and his life revolved around it. Now, six years after he joined and five years since he married Wyoming, his world was changing again. This time it was for the better. He was going to be a family man. Strange words for him, but that's what he wanted now. He wanted to be home with his family and help raise their children.

His thoughts popped like a bubble around him as Wyoming's face contorted with pain and she leaned forward. "Jeffrey…"

"What's wrong?" He tightened his arm around her, keeping her on her feet.

"It's time…" A moan stretched out in the stillness.

"What? Now?"

She didn't answer as she breathed through the contractions but as they passed, she nodded. "It started before we left Lynn's, but I didn't want to spoil the evening. We're about to be parents…"

 *Epilogue*

In the three months since they'd moved, things had been going smoothly. Wyoming and Jeffrey were closer than ever before, even closer than when they were first married. She came to realize that the man she fell in love with had more sides to him than he ever let on. He had an attention to detail when it came to restoring houses that she would have never believed if she didn't see it for herself.

Larson and Rayleigh were the sweetest babies she could have asked for, and besides a midnight feeding, they slept through the night. Unlike all of the horror stories she heard about when she was pregnant, motherhood was turning out to be easy. Judy warned her that things could change in a moment's notice and the twins' sleep schedule could turn suddenly. Even if they were fussy babies, she wasn't alone. Jeffrey was there any time she needed him, and he even got up with them in the middle of the night.

As she stood here in the nursery, she realized how lucky she was. A year ago, she thought her life was falling apart and that she was losing her husband. She never could have pictured that they'd be where they were and as happy as they were. She only wished that her parents could see her happiness and be supportive. While she doubted it was possible, she would hold out hope that one day her mother would go back on her medication and be part of their lives again.

"What are you doing?" Jeffrey came up behind her, slipped his arms around her waist, and nuzzled her neck. "I thought you were done watching them sleep."

"I am." She kept her voice low so she wouldn't wake the kids.

"She's okay. The doctor gave her a clear bill of health weeks ago. Stop worrying."

Her gaze landed on their little girl. They knew they wanted to name their son after Jeffrey's father and grandfather, giving them the perfect name of Larson, both of their middle names. They hadn't decided on a name for their daughter and had thought they had time once he came home from deployment. Their children had a timing all their own and they were unwilling to wait another day.

The birth had been rough but she hadn't realized how bad things were until Rayleigh was born. While Larson had been ready to come into this world, kicking and screaming, she was hesitant. She fought every push and managed to wrap her umbilical cord around her neck. They almost lost her.

As the sun broke over the horizon, Wyoming and Jeffrey had been forced to watch as the doctors fought to save their daughter. It seemed like the longest minutes of her life and her complete helplessness weighed on her shoulders. Jeffrey held her hand and comforted her, as there was nothing else they could do. But as her cries joined in with Larson's, she turned to Jeffrey with the first name that came to her. *"Rayleigh. She's our Ray of hope and Leigh because she has your fighting spirit. We'll take your middle name, Lee, and make it Leigh since she's a girl."*

"Come on, D wants to go over some thoughts with you before she meets with Kyle and Staci about the United Homefront Ranch site. She's nervous and needs you to reassure her that everything is going to go smoothly." He slipped his hand into hers and tugged her toward the door.

"She doesn't meet with clients often, maybe…" Her words trailed off and she shook her head. "No, she'll go and she'll be fine. I used to want to spend all of my free time working because I enjoyed it, but you know what, there's more to life than work."

"I never thought I'd hear you say those words," he teased as they stepped into the hallway.

"I guess we've both changed. Funny what becoming parents can do to you." She leaned into his embrace.

"Maybe we should have some more kids then." He kissed the top of her head. "We have a huge house to fill."

"Not yet." She gave him a playful swat, hitting his chest. "I know you want a bunch of kids, but let's enjoy these two before you have me pregnant again. Plus, I'm hoping to enjoy a little more time with my husband before we're busy with a dozen kids."

"And that's why I've asked D to babysit every Saturday night. We need some time to ourselves."

She knew that he meant he didn't want things to go back to the way they were before. They'd need to work on their marriage, not just work together to raise their children. They had come a long way, but if they were going to make it, they could never forget to show each other that their love was strong. "Every marriage has its ups and downs and when you've come through that, the union becomes stronger. We're in this through thick and thin. I love you, Jeffrey."

"Oh, Wyoming." He pressed her up against the wall, dragging his hand through her hair until his fingers tangled in the strands. "My beautiful wife, I love you more than I could ever express. I'm going to spend the rest of my life proving to you that you made the right decision staying with me."

"There's nowhere else I'd rather be than right here with you." She leaned into him and allowed their lips to meet again.

Marissa Dobson

Born and raised in the Pittsburgh, Pennsylvania area, Marissa Dobson now resides about an hour from Washington, D.C. She's a lady who likes to keep busy, and is always busy doing something. With two different college degrees, she believes you are never done learning.

Being the first daughter to an avid reader, this gave her the advantage of learning to read at a young age. Since learning to read she has always had her nose in a book. It wasn't until she was a teenager that she started writing down the stories she came up with.

Marissa is blessed with a wonderful supportive husband, Thomas. He's her other half and allows her to stay home and pursue her writing. He puts up with all her quirks and listens to her brainstorm in the middle of the night.

Her writing buddy Pup Cameron, a cocker spaniel, is always around to listen to her bounce ideas off him. He might not be able to answer, but they're helpful in their own ways.

She loves to hear from readers so send her an email at marissa@marissadobson.com or visit her online at http://www.marissadobson.com.
Born

Other Books by Marissa Dobson

Alaskan Tigers:

Tiger Time

The Tiger's Heart

Tigress for Two

Night with a Tiger

Trusting a Tiger

Alaskan Tigers Box Set Volume One

Jinx's Mate

Two for Protection

Bearing Secrets

Tiger Tracks

Healing the Clan

Alaskan Tigers Box Set Volume Two

Her Black Tiger

Forever Creek Shifters:

Forever Fight

Crimson Hollow:

Romancing the Fox

Loving the Bears

A Lion's Chance

Swift Move

Stormkin:

Storm Queen

Reaper:

A Touch of Death

SEALed for You:

Ace in the Hole

Explosive Passion

Operation Family

Marine for You:

Lucky Chance

Back from Hell

A Marines Second Chance *Crossover to the SEALed for You series

Beyond Monogamy:

Theirs to Treasure

Cedar Grove Medical:

Hope's Toy Chest

Destiny's Wish

Leena's Dream

Fate:

Snowy Fate

Sarah's Fate

Mason's Fate

As Fate Would Have It

<u>Half Moon Harbor Resort:</u>

Learning to Live

Learning What Love Is

Her Cowboy's Heart

Half Moon Harbor Resort Volume One

<u>Clearwater:</u>

Winterbloom

Unexpected Forever

Losing to Win

Christmas Countdown

The Surrogate

Clearwater Romance Volume One

Small Town Doctor

<u>Stand Alone:</u>

SEALed Rescue

SEALed in Texas

Starting Over

Secret Valentine

Restoring Love

www.ingramcontent.com/pod-product-compliance
Lightning Source LLC
Chambersburg PA
CBHW020641130626
46552CB00003B/1350